The Servant and the Water Princess

A Story of Ancient India

by Jessica Gunderson

illustrated by Caroline Hu

PICTURE WINDOW BOOKS
Minneapolis, Minnesota

Editor: Julie Gassman
Designers: Tracy Davies and Hilary Wacholz
Art Director: Heather Kindseth
Managing Editor: Christianne Jones
The illustrations in this book were created with
brushed pen and ink.

Picture Window Books
151 Good Counsel Drive
P.O. Box 669
Mankato, MN 56002-0669
877-845-8392
www.picturewindowbooks.com

Printed in the United States of America.

All books published by Picture Window Books
are manufactured with paper containing at least
10 percent post-consumer waste.

Library of Congress Cataloging-in-Publication Data
Gunderson, Jessica.
The servant and the water princess/ by Jessica
Gunderson; illustrated by Caroline Hu.
p. cm. — (Read-it! chapter books. Historical tales)
Includes bibliographical references.
ISBN 978-1-4048-5225-9
1. India—History—To 324 B.C.—Juvenile fiction.
[1. India—History—To 324 B.C.—Fiction.] I. Hu,
Caroline, ill. II. Title.
PZ7.G963Sf 2009
[Fic]—dc22
                                        2008032430

Table of Contents

Words to Know

caste: a class or category in which Indian people are divided

challenged: invited someone to fight or try to do something

chortled: chuckled

dharma: rules for a class

harem: area of an ancient Indian palace where only women live

occupation: job

sari: a long piece of light material worn wrapped around the body and over one shoulder

surveyed: looked over completely

waddled: walked awkwardly, taking short steps and swaying from side to side

Pronunciations

Ambu: AHM-boo

Brahman: BRAH-muhn

Dharma: DAR-muh

Geet: GEET

Kshatriya: kshuh-TREE-uh

Lakshmi: LAHK-shmee

Matsendra: maht-SEN-druh

Nirupa: nee-ROO-pah

Sudra: SOO-druh

Vaishya: VEYESH-yuh

4

India, 76 B.C.

All my life I have been a servant to
Princess Lakshmi. I comb and braid her
hair, spray her with perfume, and fan
her when she is hot.

I was born to be a servant. I was
born into the third class, or caste, called
Vaishya.

Lakshmi was born a Kshatriya, the royal caste. I will never be a Kshatriya, not in this lifetime, anyway.

Lakshmi and I live in the royal harem. All the king's wives and daughters live there, too. No men are allowed into the royal harem, except for the king and his guardian.

"More perfume, Ambu," Lakshmi commanded me one morning. It was early, but it was already hot.

I hurried to her with the perfume, then stopped. "But Lakshmi, we haven't had our baths yet!" I cried.

She shrugged. "The dirty pool water won't wash off the scent. Besides, there's always more perfume!"

The harem courtyard bustled with maids and princesses. The king's wives sat beneath shade trees to keep cool. Lakshmi's mother, the king's third wife, smiled at her.

"I wish I had a mother," I said. "Or a father."

My mother died when I was a baby.

My father was still alive, but I had never
met him. Harem girls, even servants,
were not allowed to speak with men
other than the king and his guardian.

Lakshmi was my only family, but we
were not related. She treated me
like a sister, even though I was a lower
class. We even looked like sisters.

If I wore a jeweled sari and painted my face, I would almost look like her. Almost. But I was plain and she was beautiful.

Lakshmi reached out to stroke her pet goose, Geet. All the princesses had pet geese, but Geet was the wildest. He loved to misbehave.

"Geet!" Lakshmi scolded as Geet lifted his head to nibble at her braids. He squawked in delight and waddled off.

"You naughty goose!" I called after him.

Just then, a bell rang out. The queen, the king's first wife, strode into the courtyard. Her sari twinkled with jewels.

"Today we will bathe in the river," she announced.

Lakshmi and I stared at each other in surprise. We had never bathed in the river.

"I am afraid, Ambu," Lakshmi said after the queen was gone. "The river is deep. And I don't know how to swim."

"I do. My name means 'water.' The water and I are friends. It will be fine," I said.

The king's wives led the way out of the harem and down the path to the river. The princesses and servants followed behind.

Geet waddled after us. "You stay here!" I told him as I shut the courtyard gate. He looked at us with disappointment.

On the way to the river, everyone chattered excitedly. Everyone except Lakshmi.

"Do not be afraid," I told her. "I will keep you from drowning."

At the river, I dove in and splashed around. Lakshmi dipped her toe into the water, but she would go no further.

On the way back to the harem,
Lakshmi and I trailed behind the others.

"I don't want to be afraid of the
water," she said, looking back at the
sparkling river.

Then I heard a shout. And a whoop.
And a splash.

Across the river, a group of boys were
running and jumping into the water.
They swam like fish, diving and flipping
in the waves.

Lakshmi turned to me. A smile spread across her face. "I want to learn to swim like that. I want to be a water princess! And you will teach me."

"Teach you? But the palace pool is too shallow," I said.

Lakshmi shrugged. "Then we will sneak to the river. We can escape the harem at night, when everyone is asleep."

"Escape? How?"

She grinned. "You will find a way."

CHAPTER TWO
The Wild Goose Chase

The harem was quiet. It was late at night. The king's nightly visit was over, and now everyone was fast asleep.

Everyone except Lakshmi and me and the servants, who were cleaning up after the feast.

Geet stumbled to and fro, pecking at the ground for scraps of food.

"Have you figured out an escape plan yet?" Lakshmi asked.

I sighed. "No. We'll never get past the guards."

Female guards surrounded the harem, protecting us from intruders. They were armed with bows and spears. They didn't let anyone in or out.

The courtyard gates opened. The servants were about to roll out the empty food carts, as they do every night.

Geet honked and flapped his wings excitedly. He waddled after the carts, heading toward the open gates.

"Stop him!" Lakshmi yelled.

Nirupa, the head guard, reached for him. He pecked at her wrists.

Another guard dove at him, but Geet
jumped away. His honk sounded like
laughter. "Ha! Ha! Ha!" he honked.

Soon the carts were abandoned as
guards and servants chased after the
goose. Every time a guard reached
to grab him, she was left with only a
handful of feathers.

"He wants to get out just as much as we do," Lakshmi said, watching him.

Geet clucked with glee as he raced around the courtyard. Finally, Nirupa grabbed hold of his legs. She swung him upside-down as she carried him toward us.

"Every night it is the same thing!"
she said, tossing Geet at Lakshmi's feet.
"Next time I'll boil him for supper!"

Geet ran to a quiet corner of the
courtyard and smoothed his feathers
with his beak. Then he leaned against
the wall and fell fast asleep.

The servants returned to the food carts and rolled them out the gates.

I grinned at Lakshmi. "I have an idea," I said.

The next night, Lakshmi and I waited in the shadows while the servants cleaned up the feast.

Geet shuffled around us, pecking at
the ground and eyeing the food carts.
He crept up behind the servants. When
the gates opened, Geet did exactly what
I hoped he'd do. He dashed toward the
gates.

"Stop him!" cried Lakshmi.

Clouds of dust rose as the servants and
guards ran to catch the goose.

"Let's go!" I whispered.

We scrambled toward the abandoned food carts. We chose one and hid under the cloth that covered it. A shelf above the wheels was just big enough to hold both of us.

We held our breaths, listening. Geet
squawked and flapped his wings. The
guards shouted angrily. Lakshmi giggled.

Then there was silence. "I got you, you
silly goose!" Nirupa said.

"Hang on," I whispered. The servants
returned to the cart. It began to roll.

When the cart finally stopped, I
lowered my head and peered out.

"No one's looking. Let's go!" I said.

We dropped to the ground and rolled away from the cart. Then we ran out the palace doors and into the trees beyond.

"You did it, Ambu!" Lakshmi said when we were far from the palace. "I knew you'd find a way."

"Don't praise me yet," I told her. "We still have to get back in."

CHAPTER Three

The King of the Fishes

The full moon was reflected on the waves of the river. Lakshmi and I waded out to where the water was up to our waists.

"We'll start here in the shallow water," I said.

She shivered. "I hate to admit it, but I'm still scared."

I was scared, too. I was proud that my plan worked, but I was frightened of getting caught. I knew that what we were doing was wrong.

I always tried to live my life according to the dharma, the rules for my caste. If I obeyed the dharma, I might be reborn in my next life as a Kshatriya instead of a Vaishya. Now, I was afraid I'd never be a Kshatriya.

"Lie on your back," I told Lakshmi. "You will learn to float."

She tried, but she sank right away.

"I am too heavy," she moaned.

"Pretend that you are lighter than the water," I told her. "Let the water lift you up."

She tried again. "It's working!" she said, floating on her back. The moment she spoke, she sank again.

"Keep the thought in your mind," I said. "You are lighter than water."

Soon she was floating on the surface of the water. Lakshmi was as beautiful as a lotus flower floating in the moonlight.

Later, we dried off and headed back to the palace.

"You are the smartest servant ever," Lakshmi said. "Now, how will we get back into the harem?"

"We'll just climb the banyan tree outside the courtyard. Then we can drop down on the other side of the wall. But we have to be quiet so the guards don't hear us."

Lakshmi shook her head. "I don't know how to climb a tree! I am too scared."

I thought for a moment.

"The food carts will be rolled back into the harem for breakfast," I said. "We'll crawl under them and wait. We'll ride them in just as we rode them out."

"You are so smart, Ambu," Lakshmi said, smiling her beautiful smile.

I smiled, too. I might not be beautiful like Lakshmi, but I was smart.

Every night we returned to the river. Geet helped us, honking and running when the courtyard gates were opened. He seemed to think it was a game. Once, I even thought I saw him wink at me.

Soon Lakshmi could swim just as fast as I could. We chased each other from one side of the river to the other.

During those moments, I forgot that she was a princess and I was a servant. I forgot that she was Kshatriya and I was Vaishya.

Even though I loved swimming with Lakshmi, I knew it was wrong to sneak out of the harem. I wanted our river visits to end.

"You know how to swim now. Let's stop coming here. Please," I begged.

Lakshmi shook her head. "Not yet. I love the water!"

One night as we twisted and turned in the waves like tadpoles, I heard shouts.

"It's the boys!" I exclaimed. "We must hide!"

But there was no place to hide. The boys shouted when they saw us. They jumped in the water and swam toward us.

"What are you doing here?" one of the boys asked.

"Who are you?" Lakshmi retorted.

I tugged Lakshmi's arm. "We shouldn't be speaking to them," I whispered.

But she ignored me.

The boy grinned. "I am Matsendra, king of the fishes. I am the best swimmer in the river. I am the water king."

Lakshmi tossed her wet hair. "And I am the water princess."

The boys laughed.

"You are no water princess," Matsendra said. "You could never beat me."

"Meet us here tomorrow night," Lakshmi challenged. "And you will see that I can beat you a thousand times over."

Matsendra nodded. "Tomorrow night," he said.

"If you win the race, will we finally
stop coming to the river?" I asked
Lakshmi as we walked back to the
harem.

Lakshmi sighed. "Yes, yes. If I win, we
will stop sneaking out. I promise."

CHAPTER Four

The King's New Guardian

The next night, the king was late. The sun had gone down, and the food was cold. But he still hadn't arrived for his nightly visit.

"Why tonight?" moaned Lakshmi. "We'll never make it to the river on time."

The princesses always dressed up for the king's visit. Lakshmi wore a jeweled sari and gold hoops in her ears. Her face was painted. She looked beautiful.

But I realized she was just as beautiful right after swimming. She was lovely without makeup, her wet hair long and flowing.

"Where is the king?" I wondered. I wanted with all my heart for Lakshmi to win the race. I wanted to stop breaking the rules. I wanted us to stay safe inside the harem with the other girls.

Lakshmi grabbed me by the arm and pulled me toward the gates. "Maybe there will be a chance to slip out," she said.

Geet followed, his hungry beak open and reaching for Lakshmi's braids.

"But we'll miss the king's visit!" I said.

Lakshmi shrugged. "So? He's here every day."

"But he's your father!" Hot tears slipped from my eyes before I could stop them. "You don't know how lucky you are to have a father. And you'd rather go swimming than see him!"

"After tonight, I'll never swim again!" Lakshmi said angrily.

I hadn't meant to make her angry. "I'm sorry," I said.

"I'm tired of being a water princess anyway," she shrugged. She looked up at the huge banyan tree above us. "Maybe I'll be a tree princess next. Will you teach me to climb trees?"

Just then, the gates opened. Geet honked.

The king strode into the courtyard, followed by a tall man who looked nervously around him.

"I have a new guardian," the king announced. The man behind him smiled.

I couldn't take my eyes off the servant. There was something about him . . . something familiar.

The king surveyed the food in the carts. "It's cold," he grumbled. "Take this away, and bring me something hot!"

The cart rumbled toward the gates. Geet waddled at the wheels.

"Oh no, you don't!" cried Nirupa, the guard, chasing him. The other guards joined the chase.

Lakshmi tugged on my arm. "Quick! Here's our chance!"

I hid beneath a cart. I heard Lakshmi following behind me. Just as she was ready to hide under the cloth, Nirupa's voice stopped her.

"Got you!" Nirupa yelled at Geet. "And now I'm going to eat you for supper."

I dropped my head and peered out.
I could see Nirupa's feet. And Geet's
hanging head. He blinked at me.

I saw Lakshmi's feet join Nirupa's.
"You can't eat him. He's my pet,"
Lakshmi said.

Geet's head swung away as Lakshmi
took him from Nirupa. Then she set the
goose on his feet and bent down to pet
him. She looked under the cart at me.

"Swim for me," she whispered.

"Look! It's the water princess!" Matsendra chortled when he saw me at the river's edge. "Where is your little helper?"

I lowered my head to hide my surprise. How could they mistake me for Lakshmi? She was beautiful, and I was plain.

But maybe I wasn't so plain after all.

"You'll race each of us," Matsendra
explained. "If you beat all the other boys,
then you will race me."

I glanced at the boys. They looked big
and strong. How would I ever beat them?

I stepped into the water beside the
smallest boy. I tried to pretend it was
Lakshmi beside me, not the sneering boy.

"Ready. Set. Go!" Matsendra yelled.

I dove into the water. Once I was in the waves, I forgot all about the boy beside me. I forgot all about the race. I just swam.

When I emerged on the other shore,
I saw that the boy was far behind me. I
had beaten him.

One down, three to go. And then I would race Matsendra, the river king.

I beat all three boys easily.

Matsendra stood on the shore with his arms folded. "These boys are slow. They are easy to beat," he said. "But you will never beat me! I am the king of the fishes. I am the fastest swimmer this side of the great mountains!"

We took our places at the water's edge.
My heart beat as fast as Geet's wings.

"Go!" shouted one of the boys.

I plunged into the water, kicking my
feet as quickly as I could. I felt Matsendra
swimming beside me. Then he was
ahead of me.

I'll never beat him, I thought. Then I erased the idea from my mind. I was part of the water. I was like a fish. I was Ambu, water princess.

Before I knew it, I reached the opposite shore. Matsendra was nowhere to be seen. The other boys were silent.

"Where is he?" I asked.

Then Matsendra's head bobbed from the waves. He was still in the middle of the river.

I had beaten him.

When he saw me, he cried out. "No! I lost!"

"You have won, water princess!" one of the boys called to me. "You are the fastest swimmer on this side of the great mountains!"

I rushed back to the harem. I couldn't wait to tell Lakshmi about my victory.

I didn't wait beneath the carts like Lakshmi and I usually did. Instead, I climbed the tall banyan tree. When I dropped to the other side, I saw Lakshmi waiting for me. Geet was sitting at her feet.

"I knew you could do it!" Lakshmi exclaimed when I told her I won. "And now I have something to tell you."

What can be more important than the race? I wondered.

"The king's new guardian came to me. He was looking for you."

"For me?" I asked.

"Yes. He was looking for his daughter."

I slowly shook my head. "I don't understand."

"You, Ambu. You are his daughter!"

I felt my heart trembling in my chest. "He . . . he's my father?"

"Yes. And he will be back tomorrow. And the next day. And the next."

Tomorrow?

"You promised to teach me to climb the banyan tree tomorrow," said Lakshmi.

Yes. Tomorrow I would teach Lakshmi to climb trees. And tomorrow I would meet my father. Tomorrow would be a good day.

Afterword: Harem Life

Ancient Indians lived according to the Hindu caste system. People were divided into castes, or classes, based on their wealth and occupation.

The Brahmans were the highest caste. Brahmans were often priests and spiritual leaders. The Kshatriyas were the second caste. Kshatriyas were rulers and warriors. The third caste was known as the Vaishyas. Vaishyas were merchants, farmers, and servants. The Sudra caste was the lowest class. Sudras were servants and laborers.

In ancient India, Kshatriya kings lived in royal palaces. A king had many wives. His wives and daughters lived in the royal harem. It was a special section in the palace. Female warriors guarded the harem. No men were allowed in the harem, except for the king and his guardian.

Harem women spent most of the day on their beauty routine. They took baths and adorned themselves with perfume.

The princesses and wives each had a servant who styled their hair. Servants often drew fancy designs on the faces and shoulders of the harem women. They used red, white, or black paint for these designs. Married women wore a dark beauty spot on their foreheads.

The harem women spent these great lengths time on their beauty in order to impress the king. The king came to the harem for nightly visits. The king and his wives often had large feasts accompanied by music. All the musicians in the harem were female. They played harps, wooden flutes, and drums. Sometimes dancers performed for the king and the harem.

On the Web

FactHound offers a safe, fun way to find Web sites related to topics in this book. All of the sites on FactHound have been researched by our staff.

1. Visit *www.facthound.com*
2. Type in this special code: 1404852255
3. Click on the FETCH IT button.

Your trusty FactHound will fetch the best sites for you!

Look for more *Read-It!* Reader Chapter Books: Historical Tales: